Sid-cam

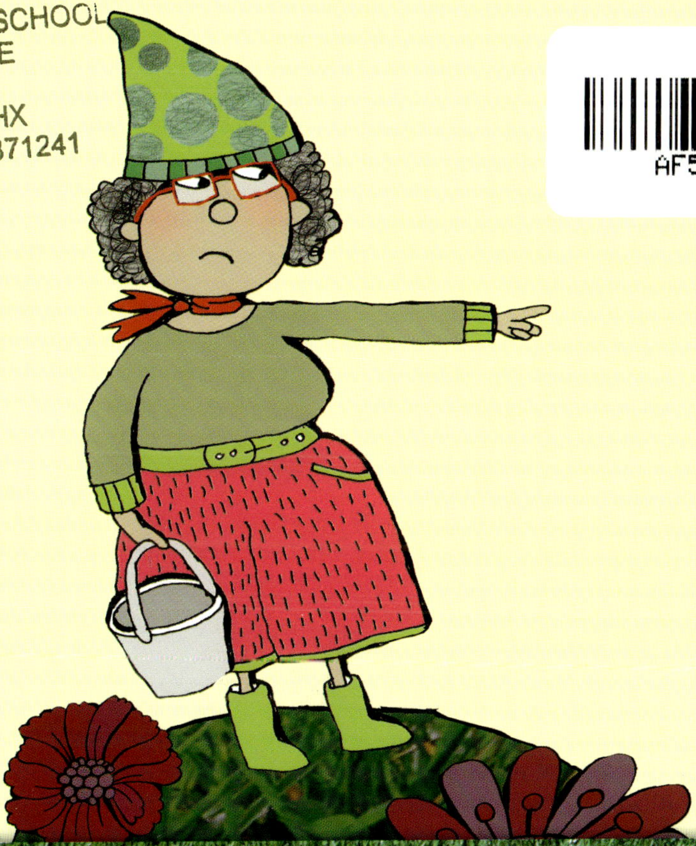

Written by Jan Burchett and Sara Vogler
Illustrated by Jess Mikhail

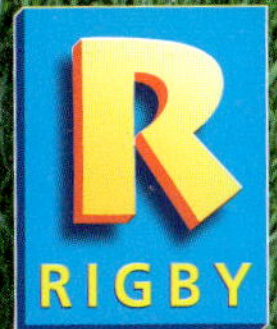

I am Sid.
This is my Sid-cam.

Join me in the garden.
It is dark.

But I can turn on my torch.
Now we can see.

Let's look for things in the garden.

Can you see the lights?

Wow! It is a star ship from Mars!

Look, they will not hurt me!

Can you see that thing lurking in the garden? Wow! It is a yowling thing from Mars.

Look, it will not hurt me!

Can you see the big, prowling thing?

The big, prowling thing with the fin …

Look, the big, prowling thing is pointing at me!

Run! It is a Nan shark from Mars!

Go to bed, Sid!

Play